SANTA CLAUS
and the
THREE BEARS

written by **Justine Korman**

illustrated by **Cathy Beylon**

inchworm
PRESS™

New York

Copyright © 1997 Inchworm Press, a division of GT Publishing Corporation.
Illustrations copyright © 1997 by Cathy Beylon.
All rights reserved.
Designed by Lara S. Demberg.
No part of this book may be used or reproduced in
any manner whatsoever without written permission from the publisher.
For information, address Inchworm Press,
16 East 40th Street, New York, New York 10016.

Once upon a time there were three bears who lived in a cozy cottage in the woods. It was Christmas Eve, and the bears were busy.

Mama Bear was baking a giant batch of cookies for a big party the next day. Papa Bear was hanging stockings by the fire. And Baby Bear was making a sign to go with the plate of cookies the bears always left for Santa.

Papa Bear sighed. "If I had a hammer I could hang these stockings right."

"And you could fix Baby's chair," Mama Bear added.

"And build me a sled," Baby Bear chimed in.

His parents laughed. Baby Bear had been wishing for a sled all winter.

Baby Bear added a picture of his dream sled to the "For Santa" sign.

"You can never drop too many hints," he explained.

Mama Bear smiled. She was sure Santa would bring a sled for her good little bear.

Then Mama Bear said, "Uh, oh. We need to go to the store. We don't have enough porridge for breakfast tomorrow."

Papa Bear and Baby Bear didn't know how to tell her that the porridge was always too hot or too cold. They were afraid to hurt her feelings.

So they got ready to go to the store.

"Pick up your crayons and paper," Mama Bear said.

"What about the plate of cookies for Santa?" Baby Bear asked.

"We'll set Santa's plate out when we get home," Papa Bear said.

For Santa

It was a beautiful night and the bears enjoyed wishing all of their forest friends "Merry Christmas."

As usual, Baby Bear only wanted to talk about one thing. He said, "If I had a sled, I could use it to carry bags home from the store."

"If I had tools, I could put a lock on our cottage,"
Papa Bear said. "Then we wouldn't have to worry
about that rude little girl breaking in again."

Mama Bear said, "And if I had a porridge maker,
I could make perfect porridge every time."

Papa Bear and Baby Bear smiled.

Soon, the Bears were back home with their porridge.
Right away, they knew something was wrong.

"Someone's been throwing our stockings on the floor!"
Papa Bear cried. He had hung them with such care and
now they were in a heap.

"Someone's been breaking my chair!" said Baby Bear.
The little chair was in pieces on the ground.

"Someone's been eating our cookies!" Mama Bear said,
examining the empty plate.

The angry bear family headed upstairs. They had a
feeling that they would find someone had been sleeping
in their beds.

Suddenly, the bears heard a deep voice that sounded
almost like... Santa Claus? But instead of HO, HO, HO,
this voice said OH, OH, OH!

"Who's that sleeping in my bed?" Papa Bear asked.
"Santa!" Baby Bear squealed. It was true!
"OH, OH, OH," Santa Claus moaned.
"What's the matter, Santa?" Baby Bear asked.

"First, a pile of books fell on me when I tried to fill the stockings," said Santa. "Then, I tried to rest on a little chair, but that fell apart. Finally, I tried to eat all of the cookies that you left out for me. I didn't want to be rude and not finish them."

Mama Bear explained that most of the cookies had been for a party, and they hadn't set out Santa's plate before they went to the store.

"Oh, oh, oh," said Santa, "I'm afraid I'm too bruised and ill to finish my deliveries."

"We'll help!" Baby Bear offered.
While Mama Bear gave Santa some bandages and stomach medicine, Santa told the bears how to drive his sleigh.

Soon, Papa Bear and Baby Bear were delivering presents all over the forest. They even brought a gift to that rude little girl, Goldilocks—a shiny new telephone so that she could call ahead before she came to visit.

For Goldilocks

When they got home, Santa was feeling much better.
He quickly hopped into his sleigh, but not before giving
three special presents to his new friends.

Papa Bear got a tool set.

Mama Bear got a Mr. Porridge porridge-maker, which made porridge just right every time.

And Baby Bear got the very sled he had been dreaming about!